This book was donated
in honor of
her 7th birthday
by
Samantha Tyson.

February5, 2004

For Rosie-jo, Scrumpy, and Ben.
—N.P.

Published by Roaring Brook Press
A division of The Millbrook Press, 2 Old New Milford Road, Brookfield,
Connecticut 06804. First published in the United Kingdom in 2002
by David Bennett Books Limited, London.

Library of Congress Cataloging-in-Publication Data

Pollard, Nik, 1970—
The River / Nik Pollard.
p.   cm.
Summary: Describes the sights and sounds of a river, from its source
high in the mountains to the place where it meets the sea.
[1. Rivers—Fiction. 2. River life—Fiction.] I. Title.
PZ7.P7583 Ri 2003
[E]—dc21   2002023138

ISBN 0-7613-1778-3 (trade)
2 4 6 8 10 9 7 5 3 1

ISBN 0-7613-2858-0 (library binding)
2 4 6 8 10 9 7 5 3 1

Printed in Hong Kong
First American Edition 2003

The River

Nik Pollard

Roaring Brook Press
Brookfield, Connecticut

Way up high,
clouds scud by.

Raindrops
drip,
drip, drop.

Wind whistles,
a stream trickles,

a hiker hopes
the rain will
stop.

Ravens caw caw caw as they soar above the stream.

The water babbles, bubbles, gurgles, gushes around the rocks and through the rushes.

Cows slurp,
mud spurts,

as wheels turn
and churn.

The truck makes **splashes**
as it **dashes** across
the widening stream.

White swans
gently glide
where the
stream's flow
starts to slow.
Swallows and
swifts come
darting in
to skim
the shimmering water.

In the stream's
safe shallows,
where a
willow spreads
its shadow...

children catch
minnows!

The stream flows down to the town.

Now it is wider.
Now it is bigger.

Now it's a river.

The river sweeps into open spaces...

**where
splashing,
dashing canoes amuse
the crowds watching the races.**

Water laps with soft slop-slaps.

Hush!

A pike.
It lurks
in green
weed...
unseen.

A fisherman drops his bait into the whorls and swirls... and waits.

The river
creeps
through
city streets.
The night is
dark but the
water ripples,
glistens, and **sparkles.**

Cranes crank, gears grate, chains clank over the deep, dank water in the docks, where the grimy, noisy work never stops.

A **big ship** starts its journey as the river nears its end.

Horns sound

and little boats

bob around...

where the river meets the sea.